W9-ACJ-560

Hayner Public Library District

HAYNER PUBLIC LIBRARY DISTRICT
ALTON, ILLINOIS

OVERDUES 10 PER DAY MAXIMUM FINE
COST OF BOOKS. LOST OR DAMAGED
BOOKS ADDITIONAL $5.00 SERVICE CHARGE.

SHE DID IT!

Jennifer A. Ericsson

illustrated by

Nadine Bernard Westcott

MELANIE KROUPA BOOKS
FARRAR STRAUS GIROUX
NEW YORK

HAYNER PUBLIC LIBRARY DISTRICT
ALTON, ILLINOIS

To my sisters—
Kathleen Remaly, Mary Barber,
and Therese Cilluffo
            —with love, J.A.E.

To Becky, Wendy, and Willy
            —with love, N.B.W.

Text copyright © 2002 by Jennifer A. Ericsson
Illustrations copyright © 2002 by Nadine Bernard Westcott
All rights reserved
Distributed in Canada by Douglas & McIntyre Ltd.
Color separations by Hong Kong Scanner Arts
Printed and bound in the United States of America by Phoenix Color Corporation
Designed by Sylvia Frezzolini Severance
First edition, 2002

10 9 8 7 6 5 4 3 2 1

Library of Congress Cataloging-in-Publication Data
Ericsson, Jennifer A.
    She did it! / Jennifer A. Ericsson ; illustrated by Nadine Bernard Westcott.—
1st ed.
        p. cm.
    Summary: Four busy sisters make a mess while eating and playing, and each
one blames the others when their mother gets angry.
    ISBN 0-374-36776-0
    [1. Sisters—Fiction. 2. Stories in rhyme.] I. Westcott, Nadine Bernard, ill. II. Title.

PZ8.3.E7865 Sh 2002   2001027283
[E]—dc21

Four sisters,
    different sizes.
Four sisters,
    early risers.

AED - 2364

Pillows fly, beds bounce,
Sheets tumble, girls pounce.
Blankets sliding to the floor.
Mother standing at the door,
Hands on hips, frown on face.
"Which of you messed up this place?"

"She did it!"

Four sisters crowd the sink,
Pushing, shoving for a drink.
Grabbing brushes, squeezing paste,
Splashing water in their haste.
Washing faces, combing hair,
Soggy towels tossed everywhere.

Mother slips, gets upset.
"Which of you got this all wet?"

"She did it!"

Four sisters round the table,
Reading all the cereal labels.
Gulping milk, spilling juice,
Grabbing bowls not in use.
Burning toast, spreading butter,
Passing jam among the clutter.

Mother sits, but finds it icky.
"Which of you made my chair sticky?"

"She did it!"

Four sisters in the yard.
Four sisters playing hard.

Digging sand, riding bikes,

Twisting swings, flying kites.

Bouncing balls, climbing trees,

Tossing mud into the breeze.

Lunch is ready at twelve-thirty.
"Which of you got these all dirty?"
"She did it!"

Four sisters slurping soup,
Making quite the noisy group.
Crackers crumble, noodles slide,
Mouths are full, but open wide.
Someone burps, someone giggles,
Someone snorts, someone jiggles.

CRACKERS

Mother scowls. She's not amused.
"Which of you should be excused?"
"She did it!"

Four sisters play indoors
While their mother does her chores.
Start to argue, start to fight,
Each believing she is right.
Staring, glaring, trading smacks,
Shrieking, weeping, more attacks.

Mother wonders what's amiss.
"Which of you girls started this?"
"She did it!"

Four sisters in a huddle,
Hoping to get out of trouble.

Listing tasks to undertake,
Four heads nod,
 four hands shake.

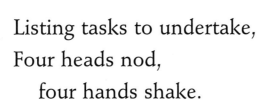

Wetting sponges, tearing rags,
Finding brooms and garbage bags.
Filling buckets, slow and steady.
Four sisters, armed and ready.

"Let's do it!"

Four sisters start to clean,
Up, down, and in between.

Making beds,
    scrubbing sinks,

Tossing anything
    that stinks.

Dusting bookshelves,

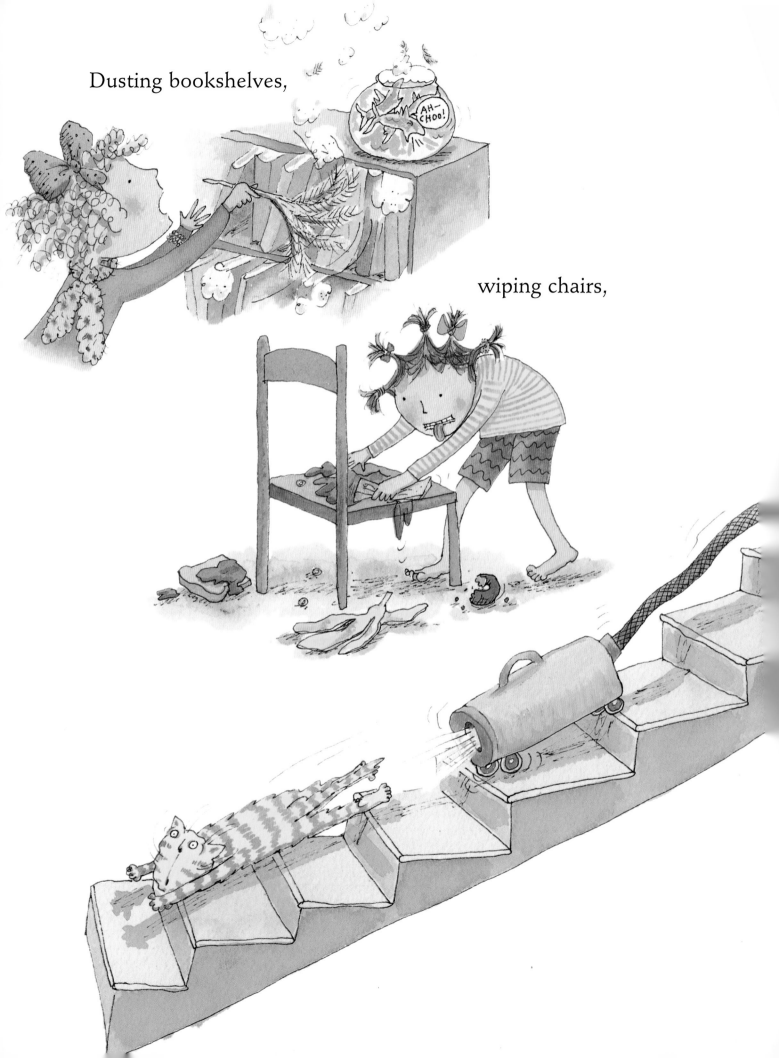

wiping chairs,

Even vacuuming the stairs.

Sponging marks,

sweeping floors,

And when their mother comes indoors,
She gasps! A smile lights up her face.
"Which of you cleaned up this place?"